HENRY HECKELBECK

Chills Out

By **Wanda Coven**

Illustrated by **Priscilla Burris**

LITTLE SIMON

New York   London   Toronto   Sydney   New Delhi

LITTLE SIMON
An imprint of Simon & Schuster Children's Publishing Division
1230 Avenue of the Americas, New York, New York 10020
First Little Simon paperback edition August 2022
Copyright © 2022 by Simon & Schuster, Inc.
Also available in a Little Simon hardcover edition.
All rights reserved, including the right of reproduction in whole or in part in any form. LITTLE SIMON is a registered trademark of Simon & Schuster, Inc., and associated colophon is a trademark of Simon & Schuster, Inc.
For information about special discounts for bulk purchases, please contact Simon & Schuster Special Sales at 1-866-506-1949 or business@simonandschuster.com. The Simon & Schuster Speakers Bureau can bring authors to your live event. For more information or to book an event contact the Simon & Schuster Speakers Bureau at 1-866-248-3049 or visit our website at www.simonspeakers.com.
Designed by Leslie Mechanic
Manufactured in the United States of America 0722 LAK
10 9 8 7 6 5 4 3 2 1
Library of Congress Cataloging-in-Publication Data
Names: Coven, Wanda, author. | Burris, Priscilla, illustrator.
Title: Henry Heckelbeck chills out / by Wanda Coven ; illustrated by Priscilla Burris.
Description: First Little Simon paperback edition. | New York : Little Simon, 2022. | Series: Henry Heckelbeck ; 10 | Audience: Ages 5–9. | Summary: On a snowy day in Brewster, Henry keeps warm with a little magic while competing against his friends in a series of winter contests. | Identifiers: LCCN 2021061355 (print) | LCCN 2021061356 (ebook) | ISBN 9781665911436 (pbk) | ISBN 9781665911443 (hc) | ISBN 9781665911450 (ebook) | Subjects: CYAC: Magic—Fiction. | Snow—Fiction. | Contests—Fiction. | LCGFT: Novels. | Classification: LCC PZ7.C83393 Hoh 2022 (print) | LCC PZ7.C83393 (ebook) | DDC [Fic]—dc23
LC record available at https://lccn.loc.gov/2021061355
LC ebook record available at https://lccn.loc.gov/2021061356

CONTENTS

Chapter 1

MAGICALLY DELICIOUS!

Henry Heckelbeck threw on his boots, ran out the back door, and jabbed a yardstick in the fresh snow. *Whoa! It's a whole foot deep!*

He raced back inside and
waited for his friends Dudley
Day and Max Maplethorpe.
They were coming over to
have an epic snow day.

As soon as they arrived, Dudley and Max kicked their boots off and hung up their jackets.

Henry smiled as Dudley lifted his nose into the air.

"MMMMM, what smells so good?" asked Dudley.

"Mom made her Magical Hot Chocolate Special," said Henry. "Want some?"

"You bet I do!" said Dudley.
"Your mom's hot chocolate is
the BEST in the world!"

Mom laughed. "How do you
know? You haven't had it yet!"

"Oh, Henry pinkie swears it's the BEST," Max cheered.

"Really? A pinkie swear?" Mom asked. "That's a lot to live up to."

Mom set three mugs on the table. Each one had a circle of red and white sprinkles around the rim.

"How'd you get the sprinkles to stick to the mug?" asked Dudley.

"It's all part of the *magic*!" said Mom.

Then she poured hot chocolate into each mug, followed by mini marshmallows, whipped cream, and a candy cane.

The kids stirred the whipped cream with their candy canes. Then they sipped the hot chocolate.

"You should get an award for this hot chocolate!" Dudley announced.

"LOTS of awards," added Max.

"Well, thank you! I'm glad
like it!" Mom said.

Henry and Dudley took
another big sip, which made
Max crack up.

"Hey, wow!" she said. "You both have whipped cream mustaches!"

The boys licked their upper lips and laughed.

Then—*slurp!
slurp!*—Dudley
finished his hot
chocolate and
pushed his mug
away. Henry and
Max finished theirs too.

"Now it's SATURDAY SNOW
TIME!" shouted Henry.

The kids jumped from their
chairs, suited up for the frosty
weather, and raced out the door.

Chapter 2

SNOWBALLED!

The sidewalk was a white ribbon of untouched snow.

"Let's make tracks!" said Henry. "But no stepping on someone else's!"

The friends spread out.

Henry
made neat,
tidy steps. Dudley
took long, giant steps.
And Max plowed her boots
through the snow, leaving
two long tracks behind her.

When they got to the park, it was already packed with kids. "What should we do FIRST?" asked Max, biting the end of her mitten.

Henry and Dudley bent down
and packed some fresh snow
together.

"Let's have a
snowball fight!"
shouted Henry.

He launched a snowball at Max. She screamed and ducked.

Dudley hurled one at Henry. *Whack!* It hit him on the back.

The snowball battle was *on!* Henry ran up a hill. Dudley stayed in the open. And Max hid behind a wide oak.

They stockpiled snowballs. Then Henry launched one from the hillside and hit Dudley's shoulder. *Thwack!*

Dudley ran
toward Henry
and chucked
one at his chest.
Thunk!

Max snuck out

from behind the
tree and pelted
one at Dudley.
Foomph! It
smacked him
in the side.

Dudley ran back to his snowball pile and threw one at Max and missed. She ducked back behind the tree.

Meanwhile, Henry slid down the hill and pelted Dudley with one, two, three snowballs. *Slap! Whop! Thwack!*

The boys made snowballs on the spot and threw them at close range. Max crept out from behind the tree and lobbed a few at the boys.

Then the boys turned on
Max and whipped snowballs
at her one after the other. She
hid safely behind the tree.
The snowballs splattered
on the trunk.

Finally the boys got tired.

"Okay, okay! Game over!" Dudley said, collapsing in the snow beside Henry.

Max peeked out from behind the tree to make sure the boys had really stopped. Then she ran over.

"Yes! Yes! I'm the snowball CHAMPION!" she cried.

"How can you call yourself a CHAMPION when you were HIDING the whole time?" asked Henry.

"I wasn't HIDING," she said. "I was being CRAFTY!"

Both boys shook their heads.

"I've got an idea," said Dudley. "Let's have a winter sports contest!"

Max's face lit up. "That sounds like SNOW much fun!"

Henry thought it sounded fun too, but after losing the snowball fight, he had a *new* rule.

"Okay, but no hiding UNLESS we're playing hide-and-seek," he said.

Then he held out his hand, palm side up, and Dudley and Max slapped it.

Chapter 3

BEST IN SNOW

Max let out a loud whistle.

"Listen up, EVERYBODY!" she called out. "The Great Snow Games are about to begin!"

All the kids playing nearby stopped and looked at Max.

One boy in a blue-and-white-striped hat asked, "What are the SNOW games?"

Max leaped onto a park bench and held up her hands. "You mean the GREAT Snow Games!" she corrected him. "They're like the Olympics . . . only more fun!"

Now a bunch of kids came over.

"Can WE play?" they asked.

"ANYONE can play!" she said. Then Max pointed at Henry. "Henry, tell everyone about the first contest!"

Henry's eyes widened. "Who, ME?"

Max laughed. "Yes, YOU!"

"Okay," Henry said. "Um, the first contest will be . . . the Silly Snow Angel. Everyone make a snow angel, but decorate it silly, and the SILLIEST one WINS!"

Kids flopped onto their backs and swished their arms and legs through the snow to make snow angels.

Henry drew a huge alien head with bulgy eyes on his snow angel alien.

Max created a snow angel queen with a crown of pine cones.

But everyone agreed Dudley made the best one of all.

His snow angel looked like it was running! It even had long hair made out of sticks, and it was jumping over a volcano Dudley made out of rocks! Plus, he gave it a really silly face.

Max wrote *First Place* in the snow underneath Dudley's snow angel.

"ONE POINT for Dudley!" she said. "You get to choose the next contest!"

Dudley's face lit up. "Okay," he said. "The next contest is Snow Fort Building!"

Chapter 4

FORT GREATNESS

The kids scrambled to build their snow forts. But not Henry. He wanted the *perfect* spot.

Dudley set up between two trees. Max picked the bottom of a hill.

Then Henry spied the playground. *Under the slide or the jungle gym might work,* he thought. *But the crawl tunnel would be perfect!*

Henry raced to the crawl tunnel and dropped to his knees.

He scooped up snow along
the sides of the tunnel and
piled more snow on top.

Soon the entire tunnel was
covered.

Henry crawled inside and poked snow out of the lookout holes on either side of the tunnel.

Now he could watch all the kids from inside his snow fort, and the best part was, nobody could see him!

I'm going to call it Fort Greatness! he thought. *I'll win this event FOR SURE!*

"Okay!" Max yelled in the distance. "It's time to vote!"

Chapter 5

SNOW-AND-TELL

Dudley went first. He made snow bricks to form a wall in between the two trees.

"My fort has a wall to protect you in a wicked snowball fight," he explained.

Then Dudley leaped over his wall and ducked down.

Henry lobbed a snowball over the top of the bunker.

Splat! It landed on Dudley's neck.

"THAT IS SO COLD!" wailed Dudley, and everyone laughed.

"So much for protection!"
said Henry, laughing.

Dudley stood up and brushed
off the snow. "Okay, okay," he
said, "so I didn't have time to
build a roof."

Max went next. She had built her snow fort against the hillside. She was standing proudly beside it when Dudley started waving his hands.

"Max!" he shouted. "Watch out!"

Max whipped around and saw a boy on a red plastic sled coming down the hill. She dove to one side. *Whump!* The sled crushed Max's fort and kept going.

Henry let out a big laugh, but then caught himself.

But Max had already heard him. She got up and narrowed her eyes.

"All right, Heckelbeck," Max said. "Is your fort any BETTER?"

Henry shrugged. "We'll see!"

All the kids followed Henry
to the playground.

"Welcome to Fort Greatness!"
he said proudly. "You can
enter—or ESCAPE—from either
end. You can also see your
enemies coming through these
special peepholes."

Henry crawled in and lay flat.

"I can't even see him!" shouted a kid from the crowd.

Then Henry crawled out the other end.

Now everyone wanted to try out Fort Greatness.

"Your fort is definitely the BEST," said Dudley, his head sticking out one end of the tunnel. "Who agrees?"

Everyone cheered except Max, who scowled. "No way! Henry CHEATED!" she said. "He used a playground structure to build his snow fort. A REAL snow fort should be made entirely of SNOW."

The kids looked at one another.

"Max has a point," said the boy in the blue-and-white-striped hat. Others agreed. Max smiled when she saw everyone was on her side.

Henry kicked at a clump of snow while Dudley patted him on the back. "Hey," Dudley said, "it's only a game. Plus your fort was REALLY cool."

Max stood on Henry's fort and spoke to the crowd.

"Since we have no CLEAR winner in this round, I'LL announce the next contest. Raise your hand if you want to build a SNOWMAN!"

Everyone raised a hand except Henry. He was still mad with a capital *M*.

Chapter 6

FEELING FROSTY

Max announced her special rules for building a snowman. "Rule Number One: It HAS to be made of SNOW. You can't pack snow around a statue and call it a snowman!"

Henry and Dudley both
rolled their eyes.

"Rule Number Two,"
Max continued. "Your
snowman has to
have an element of
SURPRISE."

Dudley's mouth dropped open. "What do you mean by 'an element of surprise'? Do our snowmen have to breathe fire? Or tap-dance?"

Max nodded. "Yup! So long as it's a surprise."

Henry shook his head. "Come on, Max. Can't we just make REGULAR snowmen?"

Max folded her arms. "What's the matter, Henry? Have you turned into a SNOW CHICKEN?"

Henry's face turned red, and Max could tell he was mad.

"Sheesh, Henry!" she said. "I'm only KIDDING!"

"So, do you have any more rules to add?" Henry huffed.

"Yes, I do," said Max. "Rule number three! The snowman contest starts NOW."

The kids scattered in a flash. Henry found an area near the woods—away from everyone else. He stopped and scrunched his fingers inside his mittens. His hands had gotten cold.

He started rolling a giant snowball for the base of his snowman, but he had to stop. His fingers were almost numb!

Aw, now I'll have to go home EARLY! Henry thought.

Then something caught his eye. A ball of light glowed in the woods. The light floated toward Henry.

It was his magic book!

Chapter 7

TOASTY HANDS!

Henry made sure no one was watching. The book opened, and the medallion floated around his neck. Then the pages began to turn until they stopped on a spell.

Toasty Hands

Are your hands frozen from playing in the snow? Have your mittens soaked through? Perhaps you're building a snowman and your fingertips have gone numb. Worry no more! This spell will make your fingers warm and toasty in no time!

Ingredients:
1 pair of mittens
A little ray of sunshine
A handful of snow

Mix the ingredients together and blow three chilly breaths. Hold your medallion in one hand and hold your other hand over the mix. Chant the following spell:

Chilly willy wee!
Chilly willy woo!
Mix your mittens with some snow,
and let the sun shine through!

Henry found a sunny spot nearby and dug a shallow hole in the snow. He plopped his soggy mittens in the hole and sprinkled a handful of snow on top. Then he breathed three puffs on the mix and chanted the spell.

A warm breeze swirled around Henry's hands. He wiggled his fingers. They were still freezing.

Then he slipped his mittens back on. They were dry and warm. Suddenly his fingers became super toasty!

Henry went right back to
work. He rolled the snowman
base, then a middle, and then a
smaller head. Next he stacked
everything together.

Now what could he use for the face? Suddenly a breeze blew over a top hat with a carrot and rocks. It was perfect!

Henry stood back and admired his snowman. The only thing it didn't have was an element of surprise.

But then Henry noticed
something really strange. His
snowman was beginning to
drip.

Chapter 8

SNOW PALS

Henry tried and tried to fix his snowman, but each time he touched it, the snow melted more and more!

Then he looked at his mittens. They were glowing!

Oh no! Henry thought. *The spell made my hands too toasty warm!*

Henry's shoulders slumped.
His snowman was a snow blob.
But at least it had stopped
melting.

That's when Dudley shouted the words Henry didn't want to hear. "Time's up! Show your snowman!"

Max, of course, wanted to go first.

She called out to the crowd, "Friends, I have not built a snowMAN, because those are BORING! Instead, I built a SNOW PAL!"

The kids all gasped. Max's
snow pal had wavy straw
hair, a pink button nose, and
a pencil in its stick hand.

"And now for my surprise," Max announced. "My snow pal is an official member of the Supreme Snow Court!"

Everybody clapped and laughed at Max's supremely cool snow pal.

In fact, everyone called their snowmen "snow pals" from then on. Henry actually liked that. Plus, everyone else's snow pals were so creative!

One was doing a headstand.
One had a surprised face with
wide eyes and a round mouth.
One was even riding a sled!

Then Henry had to show *his*
snow pal.

"Before you say anything,"
Henry said, "I already know
my snow pal is SNOW GOOD."

But the other kids didn't agree. They *loved* Henry's snow pal because they had never seen anything like it!

The comments piled up.

"How did you make this?"

"It looks like a water mountain with eyes!"

"Will you make me one?"

And just like that, Henry had tied with Max.

"This can only mean one thing," said Max. "It's time to play sled train."

Chapter 9

THE SLED TRAIN

Sled trains were fun, but they always led to snow tumbles. That's what made them *so much fun*! Max didn't have to tell Henry the rules this time. He already knew them.

Each kid took one sled. Then they held on to one another to form a train. The sled train that made it down the hill without losing any riders was the winner.

Everyone went to the top of the hill, and they were given inflatable sleds by the park rangers, who made sure everyone was safe.

Then they formed two trains:
one led by Henry and one led
by Max.

"The winners are leaving
the station!" Max said. "Go!"

Both teams started down the hill, and Henry's sled train picked up speed. *Bumpity-bump! Swoosh! Chitter-chatter!*

The riders on Max's sled train let go of one another one by one.

But Henry held tight to his
sled as he steered the train. He
was going to win thanks to the
magic warmth in his hands.

Then something happened.
Henry's hands got hot . . . like,
really hot, until—*POP!*

Henry's sled burst from the
heat, and he lost control.

"It's a sled train tumble!"
somebody shouted.

108

Henry's sled train burst apart. Some kids flipped over and slid down on their backs, and some on their bottoms.

Everybody landed in a heap at the bottom of the hill.

Chapter 10

TOASTY MITTS!

Henry gulped as he lifted his head out of the snow. Had he ruined the Great Snow Games?

Then all the kids popped up . . . and they were laughing and clapping!

Even Dudley and Max burst
into laughter.

"That was epic!" said Dudley.

"You're not mad I caused the crash?" Henry asked.

Dudley slapped him on the back. "No way! The crash was the BEST part!"

Max nodded. "Yup, I have to agree. Dudley's right!"

"Should we try it again?" Henry asked.

"No way!" said Max with a shiver. "I'm FREEZING. How come you're not frozen solid, Henry?"

Henry held out his magical
mittens. "It's these toasty mitts!
Check them out!"

Dudley and Max held out
their hands, and Henry rubbed
them with his mittens.

"Whoa, you made my hands WARM again!" said Dudley.

Max's eyes grew wide. "MINE too! How did you DO that, Henry?!"

Henry winked and said, "It's a Heckelbeck magic secret."

Max picked up her sled. "Whatever it is, it means we can try another sled train. All aboard?"

"All aboard!" cheered Henry and Dudley.

Then the kids raced up the
hill to make another sled train.
And this time, everyone stayed
on track.

Check out the next book starring **HENRY HECKELBECK**

Chugga-wump-wump!

Henry could hear the frog. Now he just had to find it. He peeked in between the tall grasses and scanned the lily pads.

An excerpt from *Henry Heckelbeck and the Great Frog Escape*

Chugga-wump!

Henry slowly looked from side to side. Then he gasped. There, sitting on a large lily pad, was an enormous bullfrog.

Whoa! Henry thought. *This must be the Frog King of Brewster Creek!*

Henry crept from behind the grasses and stepped into the shallow water.

An excerpt from *Henry Heckelbeck and the Great Frog Escape*

He could feel the cold water through his rubber boots.

"I have to catch you, Frog King!" Henry whispered. "My friends won't believe it!"

He took another small step forward and raised his net. The frog didn't budge from his lily pad throne. It was going to work! Henry was going to catch that frog!

An excerpt from *Henry Heckelbeck and the Great Frog Escape*